Sparky the Squirrel

by Greg Renz

DEDICATED TO RENZ OLIVER

It was in a swamp in south Georgia by a big river. Sparky was the only baby squirrel of Mr. and Mrs. Sparks.

Sparky was a bit spunky, always playing around. But it's okay, he was little. He wasn't as big as other squirrels. But he didn't care.

He always tried harder than all the other squirrels. Mr. Sparks said Sparky was a go-getter.....whatever he told him to "go get", Sparky got.

One day a big storm came up the river and flooded all of the ground around Sparky's home. Acorns were all floating in water. All the Sparks' winter food was floating down the river. Sparky was scared. All of the winter food was gone.

Mr. Sparks told Sparky, "It's okay. We have your uncles and cousins up in the fields by the pecan orchard. We can go stay with them. We're family."

This journey would be long and hard because the ground under the trees was all water and deep. Squirrels don't like to swim. The Sparks would need to travel through the tall treetops to the edge of the swamp.

Sparky was scared again. It was really high in the treetops, jumping from limb to limb, and Sparky was new at this task. Mr. Sparks told Sparky,"It'll be okay. You have always worked hard for your family and yourself."

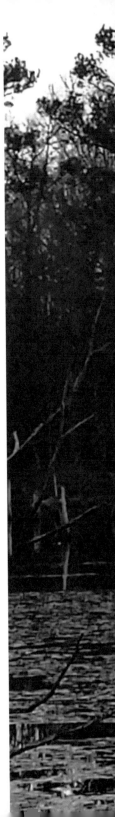

The next morning they went as fast as they could through the tops of the trees. All the way Sparky was right beside Mom and Dad. Sparky was still scared because he knew at the end of the swamp was a big treetop jump that was so far of a jump that he didn't think he could make it.

As they got to the end of the swamp, Mr. Sparks got the family to stop and rest for the big jump out of the swamp. The ridges were steep and high. Big sinkholes were there. The water in the holes was deep and swift.

As the Sparks got to the edge of the swamp, it got really windy...not in one direction but from everywhere, swirling! Sparky was scared.

His dad said, "You can do it. Watch this." His dad backed up to the tree and ran as fast as the wind and leaped to the top of the fields.

It was Sparky's turn. Mom was going last just in case Sparky didn't make it.

Sparky was scared. It was windy. His mom told him, "Go as fast and jump as far as you can. You'll make it."

Sparky backed up to the tree, just like his dad had done. He took a big squirrel breath and took off as fast as lightning down the limb.

He jumped so far he went past his dad, scared the whole way. But he made it!

As soon as Sparky landed, Mom was right behind. They were all together and the cousins were barking in the orchard. There were more pecans than anybody had ever seen.

Sparky was hungry and tired after his journey and ate so many pecans that he slept the rest of the day, dreaming of all his family and pecans.

AuthorHouse™
1663 Liberty Drive
Bloomington, IN 47403
www.authorhouse.com
Phone: 1 (800) 839-8640

Published by AuthorHouse 04/20/2015

ISBN: 978-1-5049-0729-3 (sc)
ISBN: 978-1-5049-0730-9 (e)

Library of Congress Control Number: 2015906194

Print information available on the last page.

Any people depicted in stock imagery provided by Thinkstock are models,
and such images are being used for illustrative purposes only.
Certain stock imagery © Thinkstock.

This book is printed on acid-free paper.

authorHOUSE®

About the Author

Hi, my name is Greg Renz. I was born in Athens, Georgia. Go Dawgs! I was raised in Dalton, Georgia. I grew up playing all sports, but mostly swimming and diving. Now my main passion is cooking, hunting, fishing, and gardening. Sparky was created from many hours in the swamps of South Georgia on the Flint River. I hope that this book will challenge you to overcome obstacles and inspire you to work hard.

Printed in the United States
by Baker & Taylor Publisher Services